The
Mauritius Command

PATRICK O'BRIAN

STEIN AND DAY/*Publishers*/ New York

First published in the United States of America, 1978
Copyright © 1977 Patrick O'Brian
All rights reserved
Printed in the United States of America
Stein and Day/*Publishers*/Scarborough House,
Briarcliff Manor, N.Y. 10510

Library of Congress Cataloging in Publication Data

O'Brian, Patrick.
  The Mauritius command.

  I. Title.
PZ3.01285Mau 1978   [PR6029.B55]   823'.9'14   77-26234
ISBN 0-8128-2476-8